This book
belongs to

.........................................

.........................................

GORDON'S HILL

ULFSTEAD CASTLE

FFARQUHAR STATION

TIDMOUTH SHEDS

KNAPFORD STATION

BRENDAM DOCKS

CHINA CLAY PITS

DRYAW STATION

THE ISLAND OF SODOR

# EGMONT

*We bring stories to life*

First published in Great Britain in 2019 by Egmont UK Limited
2 Minster Court, 10th floor, London EC3R 7BB

Written by Jane Riordan. Designed by Martin Aggett
Illustrated by Robin Davies  Map illustration by Dan Crisp

Thomas the Tank Engine & Friends ™

HiT entertainment    CREATED BY BRITT ALLCROFT

ISBN 978 1 4052 9311 2

70225/002

Printed in Italy

# Thomas and the Dinosaurs

This is the story about Thomas the Tank Engine and the time he came face to face with a dinosaur …

Thomas the Tank Engine liked to boast that he wasn't scared of anything.

**"Nothing scares me,"** he peeped to his coaches Annie and Clarabel. They just smiled. They were used to Thomas showing off!

James was taking some passengers to the Docks.

**"Peep! Peep!"** tooted Thomas, as he sped past.

**"Made you jump!"** laughed Thomas as he disappeared into the distance.

James was **not** pleased.

But Thomas was having too much fun.

"I'm going to give Percy a scare," he laughed to himself, when he saw Percy resting in the Sheds.

**"Peep! Peep!"**
Percy was jolted wide awake.
He was **not** pleased.

That evening, The Fat Controller had an important job for Thomas.

He needed him to work through the night, delivering supplies to the Workmen.

The sun had set and ...

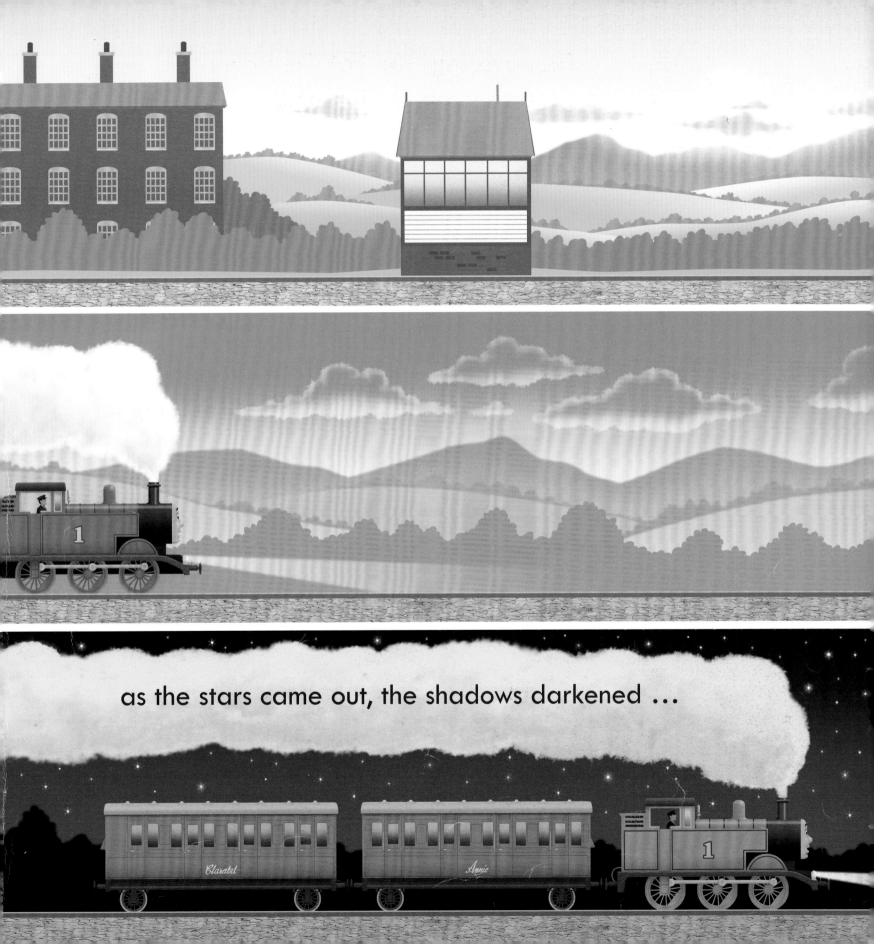

as the stars came out, the shadows darkened ...

Thomas had never been out so late before and he'd never seen Sodor looking so dark before. As he arrived at the Docks, he saw the **huge** shadow of Cranky the Crane looming over him. It gave him quite a fright but then he saw something even more terrifying ...

Out at sea, a horned creature seemed to be attacking a ship!

Thomas didn't wait to see what happened next.

**"Help! Help!"** he puffed, as he steamed

back to the Engine Sheds.

But James and Percy wouldn't listen to Thomas.

**"You're just trying to scare us again,"** they cried.

Thomas didn't sleep at all well that night.

The next night it was James who was sent out to make deliveries.

As he went past the Docks, he caught sight of a **gigantic** mouth, full of sharp teeth.

**"Help! Help!"**

he puffed, as he *wheeshed* away from the monster, as fast as he could.

Percy had heard Thomas and James's tales of **monsters**, but he didn't believe them.

**"They're just trying to scare me,"** he said to himself, **bravely**, as he set out the next evening to deliver the night mail.

But as he got close to the Docks, a **huge** shadow fell across the tracks ...

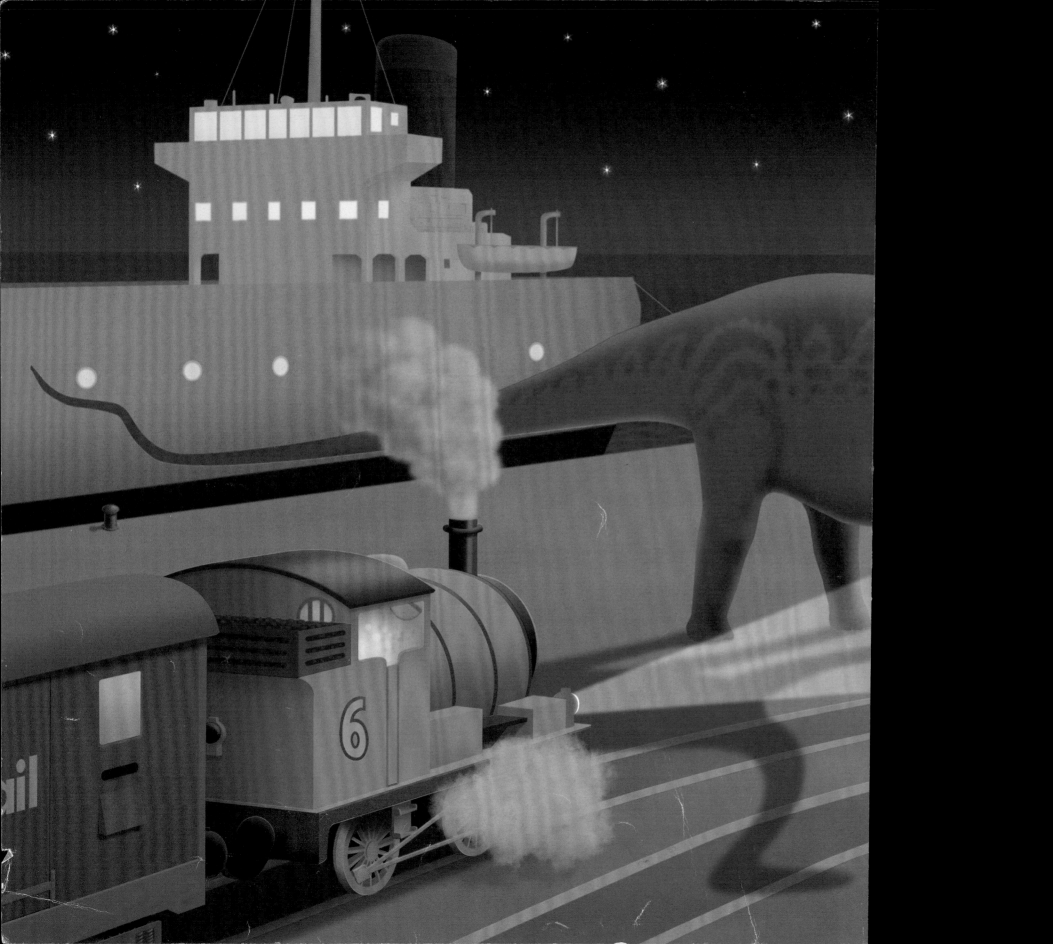

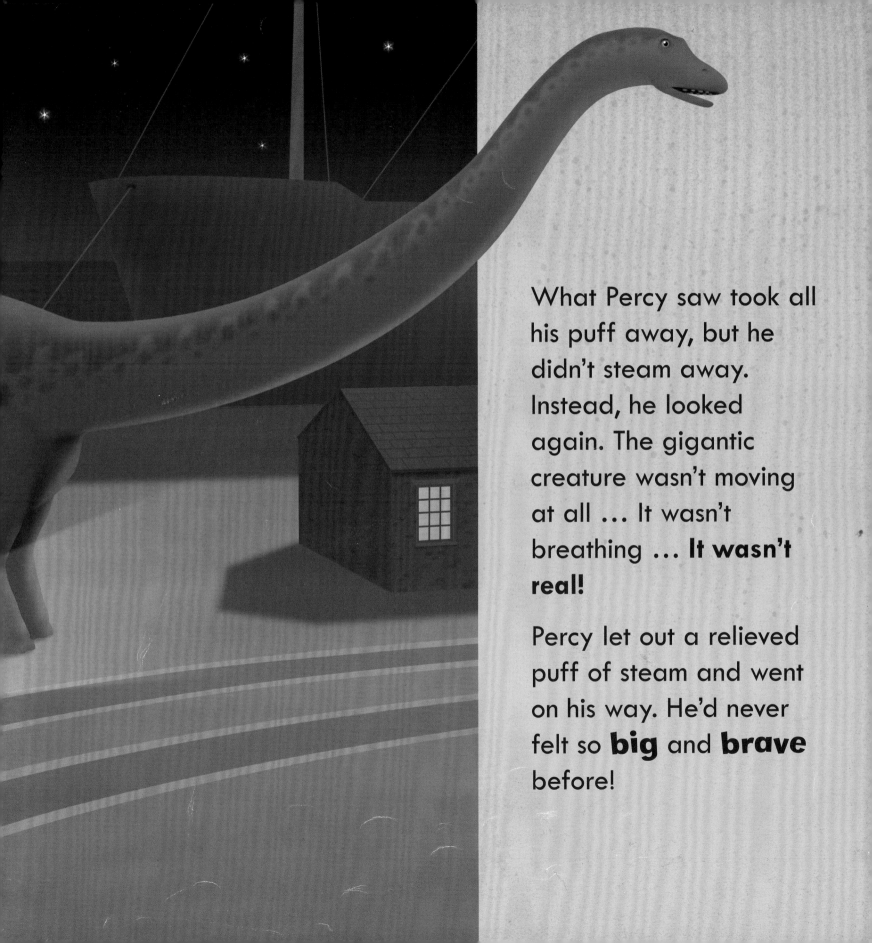

What Percy saw took all his puff away, but he didn't steam away. Instead, he looked again. The gigantic creature wasn't moving at all … It wasn't breathing … **It wasn't real!**

Percy let out a relieved puff of steam and went on his way. He'd never felt so **big** and **brave** before!

The next morning, The Fat Controller went to speak to the engines.

"I've heard that some of you have had a scare," he smiled.

Thomas and James blushed from buffer to buffer.

"The creatures you've seen in the night aren't anything to be scared of," he explained. "They're models for the new Dinosaur Park."

The engines were excited to hear about the park.

"Thomas, Percy and James, I'd like you to deliver
the dinosaurs," announced The Fat Controller.
**"If you're not too scared, that is!"**

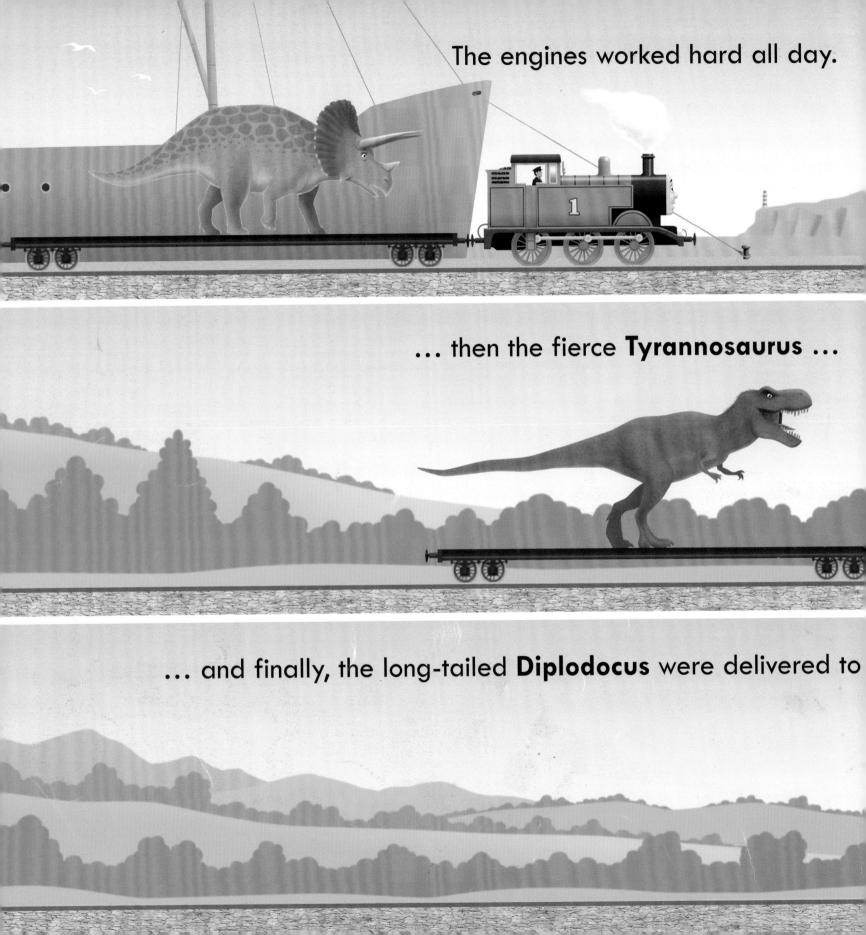

The engines worked hard all day.

... then the fierce **Tyrannosaurus** ...

... and finally, the long-tailed **Diplodocus** were delivered to

First the horned **Triceratops** ...

their new home in the Dinosaur Park.

DINOSAUR PARK

The next day, the Dinosaur Park was open to the public. Thomas was put in charge of taking the very first visitors to see the dinosaurs.

The children **squealed** and **shouted** with terrified delight.

# "There's nothing to be scared of,"
Thomas reassured them.

Percy overheard Thomas and chuckled to himself!

GORDON'S HILL

ULFSTEAD CASTLE

FFARQUHAR STATION

TIDMOUTH SHEDS

KNAPFORD STATION

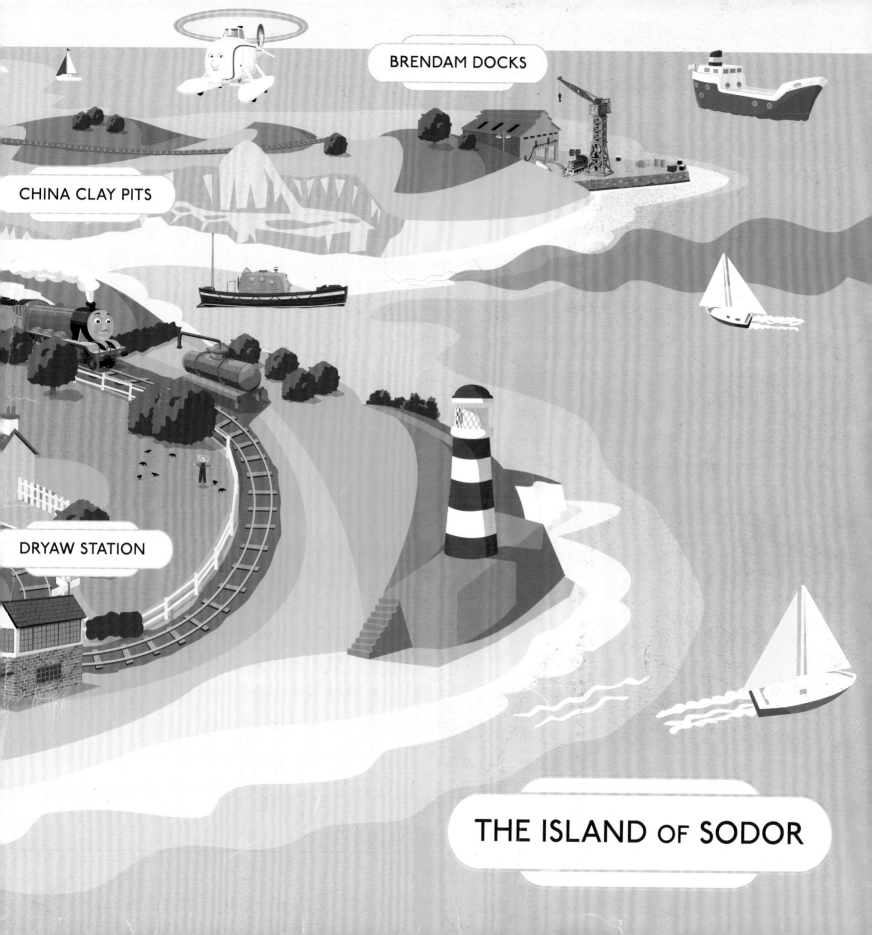

BRENDAM DOCKS

CHINA CLAY PITS

DRYAW STATION

THE ISLAND OF SODOR

# About the author

The Reverend W. Awdry was the creator of 26 little books about Thomas and his famous engine friends, the first being published in 1945. The stories came about when the Reverend's two-year-old son Christopher was ill in bed with the measles. Awdry invented stories to amuse him, which Christopher then asked to hear time and time again. And now for over 70 years, children all around the world have been asking to hear these stories about Thomas, Edward, Gordon, James and the many other Really Useful Engines.

*The Three Railway Engines,* first published in 1945.

The Reverend Awdry with some of his readers at a model railway exhibition.